THE FORBIDDEN LOVE

THE FORBIDDEN LOVE

BY

POPPY RUSERT

ISBN 978-93-5438-941-2

Published in India 2020 by Pencil

A brand of

One Point Six Technologies Pvt. Ltd.

123, Building J2, Shram Seva Premises,

Wadala Truck Terminal, Wadala (E)

Mumbai 400037, Maharashtra, INDIA

E connect@thepencilapp.com

W www.thepencilapp.com

Author biography

My name is Wendrila Kundu, 24, female. I was born and brought up in a middle class family, where career means something wich your parents say. So beeing passonate about writing, I never got oppurtunity to pursue. I have completed my graduation in hospitality sector, MBA in Hr and currently Pursuing CMA. Lost my job and found myself helpless. The love of my life, with whom i have dream to have a future today broke up with me, saying he have family issues and I am his bad luck. I lost all my friends, Lost my hope and lost my vision in life.He left me, when I needed him the most. I am still recovering. but I want to focus on studies and writing. So Please read share, like and comment your opinion. This Is my first fanatasy novel ongoing. Please share your opinion.

Contents

Prologue

Many years ago, when God created the lands and the seas, the creature and celestials or realms, god created magic, He gave the powers so, that they can create the world a better place but he saw his creations are becoming obsessed with the magical powers not for spreading good, but using for their own motives. So he took back the powers from every mortal and slowly everyone forgot about it, He then hired supreme celestial people to hold the magic he created, the world was going good until the rebel was born, there was the supreme who holds the power of FIRE, the furious and the carefree, the strongest of them all. He was the son of the SUN himself with the power of the destroyer. With his powers he quickly became the leader of the soldiers in the seven seas, and then there was supreme who hold the power of WATER, she was the favorite daughter of god, the gentle and the clam and beautiful, and the only one who can contain the power to calm the fire, with the several fights together, they fell in love each other, and then, one night the supreme of DESIRE, saw the WATER princess, and immediately had fallen for the WATER princess, but knowing her heart belongs to the FIRE prince, He and all other Supremes made strategy to avoid their being ONE. The supreme of DESIRE made many proposals to the WATER princess, but every time she rejected, in anger he and the other supreme lords created the conspiracy to kill them at once, knowing their life is at threat, they begged the Lord to give them one chance to prove their love, but then, other Supremes had pledged that they had broken the law being attracted of someone who would never go with each other and abandoned their duties and responsibilities, so they must be punished to perish. Understanding that there is no her way, God perished their souls unwillingly, but yet he gave them one more chance to show their love.

And then Once it was said, The FIRE and WATER can never be one. So to make them wrong, in the land of beautiful flowers, took birth the beautiful princess, pure in heart, the white skin, beautiful black hair, eyes feel like a lotus, lips of roses seems very fragile and sweet, the queen of Rajnagri, Devi Laxmi was a wise queen, and the king, king Druv indeed was nobleman for the kingdom, it was the dark night, with the cloud and thunderstorm, the kingdom has got their princess. it was magical all the way, it seems like the happiness came back from heaven, every people came from far lands to celebrate her birth, to see this beautiful magical princess, which brought the happiness back to this kingdom after 1000 years. These years, the kingdom had been frightened over the monstrous kingdom, Devgarh. It was said the Queen was the cold hearted woman, who feed on innocent people's blood. she had fled all the way north and west of the kingdoms and conquered them and slaughtered the innocent, only her breed who was accepted to stay in her kingdom, else the rest of the people were slaughtered for the blood. They were monsters, and cruel. People from other lands were afraid of them.

The kingdoms of Rajnagri was the purest place on the earth, the green meadows, and valleys and the beautiful flowers and the breeze all over the land seems beautiful to watch, the golden rays of the sun fall on the ground, The castle stood strong as the worrier in this beautiful land when the old saint walks in the king's court and did the prophecy of that little girl.

Old Man with his calm mind addressed the king and queen, and looked at the princess and smiled-" This little girl is the savior of this kingdom, she is a new fate, she shall hold this prophecy for giving us the new realm, and the true meaning of LOVE.

King looks confused and asked-" elderly sir, I beg your pardon, but how can she save our kingdom? she is only a little girl!

The old man smiled and said-" fool you are to think her as fragile, yet she is fragile as frost, But she had the power of LIFE. That this humankind is insufficient to hold and understand. She is the Form of life.

Queen looks really nervous from the conversation, she was afraid of her little daughter's fate and exclaimed in fear -" I beg u elderly sir, my little girl is an ordinary princess, do not let her in this fight.

The old man turned to the queen and tried to calm her and said-" My queen. she is the only hope, do not fool yourself thinking she is an ordinary girl, during her birth, she already drew the 8 celestial powerful spirits to guard this kingdom against the outside. My king, you have given us the savior. we all thank you. from now, Rajnagri is the most powerful kingdom of mortal land, and with your daughter's fate related to this, your kingdom is safe from the Devgarh. But,

The old man paused, and the king looked a bit tensed he asked-" but what elderly sir?

The old man's face turned a little pale and he said-" her powers are her enemy, people will try to deceive her for the power. once in these 17 years of her age she will meet her destiny which would turn her power so strong that her mortal body will find it difficult to hold it, and it may also cause death. she will die for her love.

The queen cried and begged the old saint-" please I beg you save my daughter's life, we cannot lose her she is our only child.

The king came down from her throne and hold the old saint's hand and begged her-" tell me, elderly sir, is there any other way I can save my child?

The old man paused for a little while and said," we cannot suppress her power. But the more people would know about it the more she will have the danger for the life. Moreover, until she is 17 years of her age, she will not have full control over her power, and after she gets married, her husband and she became one, she will know her true power. Since she beholds the power of Life, you must name her MEGHA.

King and queen smiled at each other and accepted the name given by the elderly saint.

The people of Rajnagri appreciated their king and queen for giving them their protector and they shouted in joy-: Hail king Druv, Hail queen Devi Laxmi, Hail princess Megha, !!!

After this news, the king queen broke in sadness, and King Druv, had taken a big decision, that her little daughter is not allowed ever to go out of the kingdom ever again. she should get raised right in front of his eyes, protected. And nobody will ever know about her powers. she will have a normal life. He called his true friend and the advisor of the kingdom and he passed all the orders. Also, he took the decision that his friend's son Arjun and his daughter will get married when they grew up, and will stay here forever, in this way she would not get harmed anyway.

The kingdom sealed this information from the outside world. slowly the news spread all over the world about this mysterious princess; And then this news also came to the ears of Queen Diana.

Devgarh is a dark kingdom settled in the wilderness in the dark, where no sunlight can reach. the trees were dead from the core due to the darkness in this kingdom, no new leaves would ever grow on branches, the wilderness seems scary as the dead. And the castle was settled as cold as the queens' heart guarded by hyenas and wolves

Queen Diana gave a wicked smile and said-" well, how long can they suppress the truth from us? My son is the strongest of them all, he shall take over this kingdom. And once he does so, he will win over the world. Darkness will be all over the world. No one will ever be a match for my son in front of his powers. He is no ordinary prince, he is born from the fire and ashes of the darkness. My people! I queen Diana, promise you a better future soon, living under the dark days are over, Once my son, take over no need to fear from the sun ever. We would get the equal power like the other mortals and then, no need to fear for food anymore, we shall feed on anyone, anytime, and anywhere.

The creatures stand all together bowed to the queen and shouted-" Hail queen Diana! Hail queen Diana! Hail queen Diana!

The meeting

The news spread like fire in all way, of me been missing, Soon the news also reaches out to my fathers, who broke into sadness and fear. All other kingdoms come aware that Rajnagri is no longer protected, It's like the open access to take control of, But also they aware, Queen Diana is after Rajnagri, So no one, dare to take charge against Queen Diana.

In the court of Queen Diana, she receives the news of my mysterious disappearance.

Queen Diana said to Daniel in anger-" How can this happen? She is just a little girl, And you lost her? Is this to bring me and my powers to a shame or this Arjun managed to play me?

Daniel-" My apologies her majesty, but before we reached Rajnagri, She already fled from there.

When Queen and Daniel Were talking about me, Sanjay walked into the court; And Queen stopped discussing the matter.

Sanjay asked in a hushed tone-" Who's been missing mother? Who are you after now?

Queen smiled in her dignity and replied-" Nothing that needs your attention as of now, My dear son.

Sanjay-" I heard of a mystery princess my mother is looking for, Is that true?

Queen replied-" Yes, She is indeed I am looking for, But you don't worry, Daniel got it all covered, what I was thinking, that you and Sayantika need a good vacation from the court before the marriage.

Sanjay frowned and replied-" mother, I..."

Queen said pausing Sanjay-" I know what my son wants, and also what is best for him. Hence, Mother knows the best."

Sanjay replied unwillingly-" Yes mother. Anyways I came here to inform you, that I will be off from the court for few days, I am leaving for the hunt with my mates. Also please inform Sayantika."

In no time, Sayantika entered the Queen's court. She greets-" greeting to her majesty!! his highness!!"

Queen Diana was very happy to see Sayantika, In joy, she replied-" You have come at the right time, dear. Sanjay was about to leave for his hunt with some of his friends, I was worried that you will not say goodbye to him before he leaves."

Sayantika turned to Sanjay in the worried face and said-" His highness, are you planning to go without seeing me? I have been waiting for you since last week, Now that I have come, I have something for you before you leave."

She asked her maid to bring forth a sword wrapped in a black shiny cloth. She then turned to Sanjay and handover the sword to him and said-" I have engaged my cultivated powers in this sword. This sword will never let you down and will protect you by all means."

Just then Tarun walked in, Queen Diana's youngest son. He greets all who present there.

Tarun-" Greeting mother, Greetings brother and my would-be sister in law."

Sanjay smiled at Tarun, and Tarun returns a warm smile too, He said-" I heard you are leaving for the hunt?'

Sanjay replied-" Yes brother. Till I return, You will have to look after the kingdom and mother and father."

Tarun smiled and replied-" Don't worry brother, I will take care of everything in your absence."

Sanjay left from there to his hunt, while Queen Diana, informed Sayantika and Tarun about me and my mysterious magical powers. Though Tarun did not have strong magical power like his brother, He was very cruel and clever. Queen Diana, mostly use Tarun for the spy works in the kingdom. Whereas Sayantika was the most powerful princess in dark magic in her kingdom, she had helped Queen Diana several times with her strong dark magic. Also, Sayantika's mother was a soldier of queen Diana, she gave up her life to save Sanjay at the time of his birth, while she was pregnant with Sayantika, So Sayantika also possesses half of the dark magic from Queen Diana. Hence she wanted Sayantika to be with Sanjay.

Queen turned to Tarun and ordered-" while your brother is away for his hunt, You must carry on the official work, Keep a keen eye on Rajnagri, I want that princess here in front of me. You have 1 month. Do not fail me. You know how much I hate failures

Tarun acknowledged his mother and left the court for his given duty.

Queen Diana then asked Sayantika to come to her secret chamber beneath her throne. It was a dark place where Queen Diana practise all her dark magic and summoned the dark lord. She turned to Sayantika and said-" Listen to me, my dear. You have the biggest responsibilities, As the would-be wife of the crown prince of my son, you must know a few things, My son, Sanjay is born from the blessing of the dark lord. He is not a part of the human world like Tarun, That is why his powers are stronger than anyone. Also, this is a reason, He doesn't belong a heart, He is incapable of love. You must stay patient with him, because, greater than this weak word"Love" lays the power you will hold in the future, You will be the queen of the next Dark Lord, unlimited access to your magical powers. So you must understand your responsibilities am I clear my dear?

Sayantika acknowledged Queen Diana with a smile and replied-" Yes her Majesty, I understand"

Queen Diana turned away and said-" Very good, Now I Have the most important work for you, my dear.

Sayantika spoke in her very soft tone-" Yes her majesty,"

Queen Diana Replied-" Nobody has seen this mysterious princess still now, and neither anyone knows what magical powers she holds, But as what I have heard, she created 9 celestial guards to the Rajnagri during her birth, which makes her very powerful. You should bring me the information about her mysterious magical powers. I heard there is an Old priest in that kingdom, who has prophesied about her powers to the kingdom which King Druv Has kept hidden so far. You know what to do.

Sayantika smiled and replied-" Do not worry her majesty, I shall bring the news of this mysterious powerful princess to you soon." and she left.

It has been two days in the forest I was blacked out under an old tree. Slowly I regain my consciousness and opened myself in a dark muddy forest with absolute darkness all around, It was so dark that hardly the rays of light can touch the ground. I looked around and I couldn't find my horse anywhere, Out of fear I started walking to the front not knowing where I am going to. Suddenly I heard a noise of horses from around, I quickly hide behind a tree nearby and waited to observe who is coming.

I was scared and stay hidden behind the tree for some time waiting for them to come forth. Few minutes passed, and finally, I saw few men on horses coming in a hurry, they look like they were from a royal family. I was in a confusion to come in front. So I stayed there waiting to observe more. I saw four men on horses steadily kept riding towards the north, While they were passing from the tree I was hiding, I quickly hide back again, after few seconds I turned out once again to see their status, are they gone? or still there. from the far, I could only see three men on horses, I wondered where did the fourth one go? and then in my back, I felt someone's presence, I turned back and saw a man, taller than me, in the suits of a shining knight armour, which glows like a sun in the dark forest, hairs pulled back, dark deep brown eyes locked on mine, with a sword on my throat. He asked me-" Who are you? what are you doing here?

I was scared and confused and not knowing how to act at that time, I noticed a sword in his left armour hanging, without wasting any time, I picked up that sword and hold on to him. With his keen eyes, he looked at me and said-" Beauty with a sword in hands huh? you are interesting. But no one dares to hold their sword against me, being a girl, you did, who are you?

I replied in fear-" You don't know me, let me go. I don't mean any harm"

Within no time, his friends came there, and they circled me, seeing no hope to leave from there, without my willingness, I put my hand towards them and shouted-" LEAVE ME ALONE!!!

An unknown forced worked on them, and they fall to the ground hard. But The man who was standing with the sword to my throat didn't get much affected. The rest of his team members again woke up and come towards me with their swords to fight. I hold the sword up and started fighting with them, With my knowledge to fight with the sword it was not much hard to fight with them, It took some time to fight with them, I was alone, and they were three, I started falling weak, In fear, I closed my eyes and I summoned my parents and god, and with my full force I picked the sword up and the unknown forced worked once again, this time it was so strong, It came with the strong magical water powers within me, which washed them away. It makes me so weak I feel like dizzying off. From the far I can only see, him, glowing with fire, protected himself and looking at me with keen eyes, I fell down again and blacked out once again there.

Into The Dark

With Arjun being sent to prison, I won at least one battle, The lady, Arjun's mistress, was sent home. But it was not something, to be happy about. Because my father was not happy with me going outside the castle. Father turned towards me and said-" Now that Arjun is been locked up, there is nobody to make it up for you for leaving the castle again."

I replied-" But father, I am fine, If I haven't gone outside this castle I would have never found out the truth.

My father said angrily-" The truth would have come forth by any means, for that, I cannot consider your safety my dear.

My mother speaks out in this-" Megha my dear, please understand, if we are doing something about your safety, we want your good, we don't want anybody to hurt you, my child.

I replied-" But mother, Our kingdom has been on the term of peace all these years. What are we afraid of? And I am not a kid anymore mother.

My father's voice turned down and he said-" There are certain things, you are not aware of yet.

I replied -" Is it related to any of my powers?

My mother quickly said-' Who said you all these?

I said-"When Arjun and his mistress have been discussing, they were saying about some powers that belong to me, and he wanted that. What is this all about?

My father said in anger-" There are no such things like that. Do not be fooled by that bastard. And we are not talking about this anymore." My father stood up, Followed by others' present in the court. My father said-"The court is dismissed now." And he walked away.

It is my seventeenth birthday today, Usually, on this day the kingdom celebrates very joyfully, but I guess this year is different, Arjun has been locked up, Father was sad and worried. mother is not fine either. It did not feel like my birthday today. Yet I was happy finally I had raised my voice against the lies. Shaanti came to my room and asked me-" Princess, Are you okay?

I replied smiling-" Yes dear I am.

Shaanti looked at me carefully and said again-" Then why do I find you in a worried face?

I said-" Well there is something which does bother me.

Shaanti asked -" What is it, princess?

I said-" I feel, there is something everybody is hiding from me. First Arjun said something about me having powers, which he wants, and then when I asked father about it he tried to ignore and hide something. This makes me more sure if there is something, everybody is hiding from me. I need to find the truth.

Shaanti asked me-" How are you going to find it out princess, by king's order you cannot leave the castle again.

I said-" That is something we need to find."

Shaanti said to me in a confusing face-" Well princess, There is an old man in our kingdom, known to be alive for 100 years, I heard, during your birth, he came to meet the King. I think he might know if there is anything.

I found hope at least, and I am ready to take the risk to know the truth-" Where will I find him? Help me to reach him Shaanti."

Shaanti agreed to help me, She had words with her beloved, to make arrangements for me during the evening, Father was leaving for his neighbours' kingdom today afternoon. It was the perfect timing for me to go out. As per our plan, after father left, We were ready to leave too. Me and Ajay (our guard, also shaanti's beloved) left to find the old man. Shaanti said to Ajay-" Take care of princess and yourself." She turned towards me and said-" Be safe princess, Come back soon. I will manage everything here until you return."

I smiled and looked at my castle once more before we left.

In the meantime, without anyone's notice, Arjun had made his plan to escape. In these years he made a few of his man to follow him, who helped him to escape from the prison when the king was not in the kingdom because that was the best time for him to take revenge. In the rage of revenge, he escaped to our most rival kingdom, Druvgarh.

Arjun said-" her majesty, Greetings from the crown prince of Rajnagri, I came here to make a fair proposal,

The Queen said-" Proposal? What kind of proposal shall I want to take from you?

Arjun replied smiling-" I was been betrayed and removed from the throne, all my hard work and my dreams had been destroyed by them, I seek revenge, I want what is mine, I want the throne, and in return, I will help you to conquer the other kingdoms, and will always be your slave.

The queen smiled and asked-" Why do I want to help you? I can easily get it if I want it.

Arjun said-" Not the Rajnagri her majesty.

The queen looked in confusion and asked-' Why not? don't you know my powers? I have no mercy.

Arjun said-" Rajnagri has been hiding a deep secret of its protection. I can give it to you.

The queen asked-" You would betray them?

Arjun said frowning-" They have betrayed me, her majesty. I have done so much for that kingdom, And in return, they dethroned me from my own kingdom. I seek revenge. and hence I came to you her Majesty, I know only you can give me justice."

The queen asked-" So tell me what is the secret that beholds the Rajnagri?

Arjun replied-" The princess."

The queen asked in confusion-" The princess?"

Arjun replied-" Yes her majesty, The princess is the protection of Rajnagri, She embraces magical powers, which shields the kingdom. When she was born, it has been prophesied that she holds the strong magical powers that will protect the kingdom forever, But she herself is not aware of that powers. Once she becomes seventeen, She will open up to explore her true magical power. Her power is so strong can provide life, or can take a life. She has turned seventeen today, and I also get the information that King is not in the kingdom, He went to his neighbour kingdom for her marriage proposal, after I have been prisoned. So If we can capture the princess, All the shields can be broken.

The queen was listening to Arjun very carefully, She understood, That I am that princess, whose identity has been hidden for years. She said-" Very well, I shall help you, But in return, I want your blood.

Arjun got frightened and asked-" Blood?

The queen smiled and said-"Don't you forget Arjun who we actually are, We live on human blood. But don't worry, I will not kill you now, you will serve me, as my slave."

Arjun not knowing, where he had come, in his rage of revenge and greed, lost his soul to the dark queen. The queen drank his blood and took his soul, and made him one of her slaves.

The queen asked one of his guards to take Arjun from there, and prepare to attack our kingdom.

The King of Druvgarh was once human too, he fell in love with Queen Daina, and gave his soul to her. But still, he holds somewhere humanity in him. He advises The queen to right or wrong. despite being called King of Druvgarh, he was just the husband of queen Diana. The queen runs the kingdom here. They have two sons, Sanjay and Tarun. Sanjay was the eldest son and favourite of the queen. He was born out of the dark and holds the power of fire that can destroy everything on earth. The queen had spoiled his son by giving all his darkest desires to come true. He is also the leader of the army, He had never lost any battle. the strongest weapon of Queen Diana. He was arrogant, Angry, a player of a woman's heart, and a dangerous monster. It is said that he doesn't have a heart. the heartless creature, world fear of. And Tarun, the youngest son, though he doesn't have any powers due to being born from a human soul when the king was still human, But he was clever and jealous of Sanjay, being called the most powerful. All his life, He has tried every possible way to be the favourite of the queen, but alas! she only gave all her attention to Sanjay. But Tarun has never stopped trying. The Queen's most trustable knight comes to her court and he greets her majesty.

Daniel-" Greetings, her majesty!

The queen replied-" Yes Daniel? How is everything?

Daniel replied-" Arjun had been taken care of. we are prepared to march towards Rajnagri.

The queen said-" very well, I have received the information needed, I don't need Arjun anymore. Keep him alive till we capture the princess. Also, I need more information about that mystery princess.

Daniel replied with confidence-" Yes her majesty. Shall I inform His majesty for this?

The queen smiled and said-" No I believe, you can manage this little work, No need to bring my son into this little matter. Let him enjoy his vacation for now. By the way where is my son Sanjay nowadays?

Daniel replied-"His majesty is at his palace, with his mistresses.

The king turned to the Queen and said-" Diana, He is our son, Do not only use him as a weapon.

The queen looked at The king in amusement and said-" My king, Sanjay is my favourite son. I love him. I dare not use him. He is the crown prince, I am just training him for the future. He needs to be ready for every circumstance, he cannot get weak."

The king replied-" You should also consider him as your son, before calling him as the crown prince. and as his mother, you should also sometimes consider giving him lessons of life, Like not to play with those innocent hearts. Your son only uses them as many as his mistresses for his part of a play, those innocent girls fall for him, and he turns them down, If this is the case, He shall become a good warrior, not a good King who shall look after his people.

The queen smiled a glance and replied-" My king, You are too naive, for this dark kingdom. My son is not only a good warrior but also the best for this throne. in our dark world, we don't have a heart like humans, If we have, we cannot rule this kingdom. And like me, my son, Sanjay doesn't belong a heart.

The king frowned and said-" But Diana, know that, once you had a heart that is why you loved me."

The queen replied to this-" Love is a weak word for us, my king. Well you are my husband, yes once in this lifetime, I became weak and fall for you, And I won't lie, that was the best time for me, but also I had to lose half of my powers as a punishment of this. In our dark world, We cannot be weak or we shall not rule this kingdom. My father knew I was the strongest in this kingdom to be crowned princess, Hence, I was given the throne. That was the main reason our son Tarun is not as strong as My son Sanjay.

The king's face turned down a little he replied-" Though Sanjay was not born from me, yet he is my son, I raised him, Given him all my love. He is my eldest son, I want his best to be.

The queen turned to him and said-" I know my king, You are the only human, that makes me weak. But you are my strength. Don't worry, He is the son of the dark. Nothing can beat him. For now, Our main focus is the mystery princess of Rajnagri.

Queen Diana, sent his small army towards the Rajnagri, Me not being their, present at that moment makes the shield weak that was made during my birth. they attacked the kingdom and got to know I was not in that kingdom. Luckily, Shaanti helped my mother to escape from there. She told my mother where I went. My mother got really scared and prayed about my safety. It was my mother's prayer that has saved me today. Somehow, Ajay's partner had given him the news of the palace is attacked. He told me-" Princess, the palace is attacked, we need to go to a safe place.

That time, I was scared, but I was very near to my truth so I cannot go back, and I cannot be selfish to keep Ajay here. My kingdom needs him. So I said-" Ajay, the old's man place is nearby, You need to go back to the palace, Save others. I will stay here. Once everything is fine, you can come and take me. Moreover, if they are here for me, I cannot go front.

Ajay looked confused and asked me-" But princess, what about your safety? I cannot leave you here. King shall...

I said-" Ajay, for now, your kingdom needs you. Don't worry I will be safe here. Nobody knows I am here. Go.

He left without his consent. I ride my horse towards the old man's house in the wilderness. Suddenly there was a dark cloud all over, My horse stopped in between, with unknown reason, I was scared, and suddenly he started behaving oddly and run towards the dark wilderness, and sometime later, he suddenly stopped and I fell down and I hit my head hard and I blank out.

Enlightened The Truth

After thinking all night, about what was happening to me, I finally found the courage to stand for myself. I knew, If I would confront Arjun and my father, neither of them would listen to me, rather they would say just as used to say to me since the childhood,-" You must understand, You must adjust, It's your duty and responsibility as a princess and a lady." But I do not want to hear those anymore. Now is my time to bring the change. I won't lie, I am scared; I am scared that what would they react when they hear the truth? But for the first time, I was ready to take the risk of speaking without any fear. I waited for the sunrise today, much than I had any other days in my life. Finally, after 5 long hours, I see the sunlight. I asked Shaanti to make me ready for the court today.

My father, mother, and other ministers in the court were in little shock of been called so early. I reach on time, as were others. I started speaking addressing The king and the queen with greetings with others-" Greetings to father, Mother and all who are present here.

The king replied in a frown face-" What is it that u summoned us here today?

I replied-" there is very important something I need to bring to the notice of the king and the court.

One of the ministers looked at me and asked-" Yes princess, Tell us what is the matter?

I replied-" I have also asked the crown prince, Arjun to be present here today and my maid Shaanti.

My mother replied to this-" Is there anything wrong my dear?

With this discussion, Arjun entered in his usual knight armor as if he was returning after all-night hard work. Arjun looked at me and the court and before he speaks he greets the King and Queen and other ministers present over there.

Arjun-" Greeting from the crown prince to the King and Queen, and other valuable members of the court. Greeting to the princess." He turned towards me and ask-" What is the problem princess? Why do you need to summon the court/ If there were any problems you would have asked me instead, I would have looked at that matter personally."

I smiled at him and said-" The matter I am discussing over here is about you Arjun.

The court murmured with a feeble discussion of what was going on. Arjun turned towards me and clutched my hands in anger and said-" Is it about last night? If it is, we could have solved it in the room, there is no need to inform our personal matter in the court.

I smiled confidently at him and loosen my hands from his clutch, I turned to my father and ask-" father, as the princess of this kingdom, I am your daughter at first, I know your love and trust for Arjun is undeniable, But this man is not proper for this throne, or to be my husband.

There was a hush silence all over the court, they were looking at each other. The king looks terrified with my words and asked me-" what are you talking about Megha?

Arjun quickly tried to calm the situation and turned to father and said-" I am sorry my king, That she was being impulsive and had brought this little thing in the court and wasted your time. It is nothing, Just we had a small fight, she was merely angry."

Father got a hopeful smile and said-" I understand, being from the royal family, she had got this stubbornness from her father indeed. I understand now. I see she is angry, Arjun, you must look at this matter as soon as possible.

I was standing still having a cold face to this conversation. After father finished I said again-" It is not something personal I am talking here. I am here to prove a liar. And I do have all the proof, But before that, I need everyone in this court to listen to me; once I complete, you should judge basis on that." Everybody in the court looked at me with a keen eye to get an explanation of what is going on. I started by saying-" The man you all are believing today here is a liar. He not only had lied to me but also this kingdom, to my father, who had loved him unconditionally.

Arjun speaks with anger-" What rubbish are you talking about princess? I told you we can take this to our room to sort out.

I replied with a rage-"What if I do not wish to solve it Arjun? Yesterday night you showed me, what is your true form, you may have fooled all of us till now, but not anymore. with all due respect, I shall say this to my king, you have chosen a wrong heir to the throne,"

Father replied in confusion-" Please speak clearly what is going on, and why are these obligations are you putting on Arjun?

I replied- Father, yesterday night, Arjun came to my room in the midnight, drunken state, and despite being told to leave He force on me.

My father's eyes have become furious to hear this. Arjun immediately replied-" nonsense, My king, I did not do such cheap activity princess is stating here.

Before he could finish I started speaking again-" Not only that, He even hurt me, and for that, I do have an eye witness, my maid Shaanti.

Shaanti came forth and given her statement-" Yes my king, the princess was resting, and it was the time of midnight when his majesty came in and forced on the princess, She got several hurt during this, we have asked his majesty to leave immediately, but he didn't,"

with shaanti's statement, Arjun got a little nervous. I started speaking again-" Arjun has been my first friend since I understood friendship, I have trusted him, yet he did that to me, Well, as I have been taught to adjust, I would have, But what I am going to tell you is going to shock you even more. When he left my room yesterday night, I thought to myself to sort everything, so I followed him, But I saw he took his horse and left, When I asked the guard I have been informed that he left again for Hailo village, There were few rumors about Arjun and a lady from Hailo village, I have been trying to avoid those trusting him, But He isn't the person to be trusted. Yesterday I left with him to seek the truth.

My father got scared and asked-" You left the palace?

I replied-" Yes father I did, and this is not only the first time I did so, I go often to the nearest valley, to the Shiva temple. Arjun did know about this, But I asked to keep it a secret as I didn't want you to get worried about me.

My father gets tensed hearing this he asked-" My daughter are you been safe?

I replied-" don't worry father, I am safe and hence I am here standing. But today you must know what is he conspiring against this kingdom. When I followed him to the hailo village, I found a lady, with whom he got intimated, and accidentally I overheated their conversation. Arjun did not love me, or this kingdom ever, He only wants the throne and said something about my power. And it seems the power has got him hard to differentiate between good or bad. At first, I did not want to believe my ears, But slowly I understood his intention, So without wasting my time, I returned to the kingdom and informed the court.

Arjun seems shocked and nervous and couldn't speak properly, still, he managed his words and asked me-" This is all lie. Why are you doing this princess? Don't you feel ashamed to drag the crown prince with such obligation?

I simply smiled at him and turned to father again, I said-" To prove my words I have brought the lady here, His mistress.

The guards brought the lady into the court and she kneeled before the king. Arjun was terrified of seeing her. Arjun looked at me with his blank face. Within no time, the lady accepted the truth and given all the statements against Arjun. In the furious state, Arjun clutched her hair and pushed her down, In the rage, he said-" You do not worth to be my queen. What haven't I been not done for you? And you still dare to talk against me? I have only loved you since the first. I have made plans for us, And did you see now how you have ruined it?

My father immediately stood up and roared -" Enough! Arjun you have disappointed me. Your father was a nobleman and was a great friend of mine. But you are nothing like him. guards take him to the prison.

I saw the guards dragging him to the prison and with his angry face he said to me"- this isn't over princess."

Broken Trust

Days Passed by, our lives were going on as before, It was evening when I was playing my sitar in the king's court. It was said that I played one of the sweetest and melodious sitar from far lands. When I was young, many peoples use to come from far lands to teach me sitar, and slowly I learned to be one of the best. King, Queen, and rest of all the peoples on the court are enjoying, while a gate messenger came to the king and bowed to him-" His Majesty, Greetings from the guard of northern gate.!!,

King Replied-" What is it?"

Guard replied in a worried face-"King, there is mystery death reported in towns,

the king replied with a frown-" Death?

Guard replied without any pause-" Yes your majesty, to the southeast border of our kingdom, were found, attacked, and killed.

king with a confused and angry face said-" call Arjun immediately!

Within few minutes, Arjun came inside the court, He was wearing as usual in his knight armor, and the pride on his face. He stood in front of the king and with a cold smile he greets him-" Greetings from the crown prince to the king!

King replied-" What is this I am hearing? There has been reported mystery murder around the kingdom and why haven't you been on the investigation?

Arjun seems a little offended with father's word, but he still managed his cold proud face and replied-" I was little busy with the township work, It has not been reported to me yet sir, But don't you worry my king, Since it came to my notice now, I will personally visit that town and investigate everything, And until and unless I solve this matter I shall not return to this kingdom.

My father seemed a little satisfied with his word and proudly smiled at him and given him permission to do so.

Within 2 Days he shall leave as per, the king's order. It was almost midnight, I was standing on my Balcony and staring at the moon, enjoying the light within the darkness, and was hoping someday, I get my own light to get out from this darkness ass well. With a sudden knock at the door, I came to my senses, at look at the door, Shaanti opened the door and there I saw Arjun standing. He was not in himself, He drank too much alcohol. His breath was stinking of alcohol smell. Shaanti tried to stop him from entering, But he drank too much to listen to anyone

Shaanti-" Crown prince, Please, it's not proper to come here at this time of night, Princess is sleeping.

Arjun furiously replied her-" Step aside, you are just a mere maid of the princess, who do you think you are to stop me from entering my own wife's room?

I came outside hearing noises and I replied-" I am not your wife, still, you must leave this room Arjun.

Arjun got angrier and replied to me-" What are you so proud of? Your beauty? Despite being the daughter of the king, I am the crown prince, You will always be below me. As my wife. Do you understand? And let me tell you, this beauty, is indeed something that I want, But there is more to this beauty which I want princess. What are you so proud of? Just like your father!! Stubborn.. Always giving me orders.. to crown prince.

I was shocked by his behavior, I never saw him like this, he always pays respect to my father, and me as well, then what went wrong today? Maybe it is because he drank a little too much. I replied in a confusing mind-" Arjun, What are you saying? You do not seem fine to me, you must go to your room and take a rest. Day after tomorrow you have to leave.

Before I could finish my words he burst into anger-" Leave? who are you to give me orders? Look at you, You don't even know about yourself, little princess. Giving me orders huh? Once I become the king, I will see what I can do to your little arrogant.

After finishing his words, he pushed Shaanti outside and closed the door, he came towards me and threw himself to me, He tried to force me, He holds my hands above my head, causing much pain, and tears rolled out from my eyes, then he bites me in my lips, causing the blood coming out, I begged him to leave me, But lust took him so high, he couldn't hear my voice at all. with an utter shock from his behavior and being scared, I pushed him hard out of the bed and Slapped him out of anger, This took his anger higher, He clutched my hair, and pushed me to the ground, He left in anger.

I was devastated, Shaanti came to me, and helped me to get up.

Shaanti tried to console me-" Princess, Are you all right? Should I inform the queen?

I replied-" No need, he is just maybe drunk, It's nothing, Do not inform anyone, You go and sleep.

Shaanti replied worried,-" But princess...

I replied with a cold face,"- I said leave shaanti.

She went away unwillingly, she closed the door behind me, I sat on my bed, and still thinking, what had happened, just in few minutes, my childhood friend turned into a person I don't know, Everything seems vague, My life seemed without any cause now. Being the daughter of the king, Indeed he had received more trust, Love, and faith as a son than me, My father gave him the throne, without judging him is he really capable of holding the people's fate and their happiness? nobody asks me ever did I ever want to marry him?

Thinking all this, I looked at the moon once again and in the dark, I was wondering, just one day before my birthday, how did all this happen? I must talk to Arjun once. Just then

I looked out of my window and saw Arjun, leaving on his horse. I wonder where is he heading to in this night? Is he ashamed of his behavior earlier? that is why is he leaving? Is he okay? Without a second thought, I ran towards him, But before I could reach he already left, Shaanti followed me there, and luckily, one of the night guards is her beloved, Shaanti asked in very prominent voice-" Is he left for the same village today?

The night guard looked at me and tried not to speak. I came forth and told him.-" Tell me where is he headed to brother? I need to talk to him urgently.

the night guard finally speaks but heisted a little bit-" Yes, his majesty headed to Hailo village today.

I replied-" Hailo village? I turned to shaanti and asked-" Isn't it the same place you were telling me that day?

shaanti replied-" Yes princess.

It sounds a little bit strange to me, but I still need to find the truth myself. without wasting another time I took one Horse, and before leaving I told shaanti-" Wait for me, till I return, nobody should know what happened here okay? With her promise, I left behind Arjun to Hailo village.

I rode through the wilderness very fast so that I could reach him as soon as possible, then finally I saw him, He was riding carelessly and in a hurry, soon we reached the Hailo village. I stood a bit far from him, I saw him getting down the horse in front of a house, I want to reach him, but before I could do that, I saw a lady came from inside and she hugged Arjun, He went inside. Without understanding what is happening, I decided to keep an eye on them secretly. From a broken window I saw,

Arjun kissed that lady very passionately. Both of them started getting intimated, Arjun started kissing that lady with all his passion, his hands are going all over her body and opening all her clothes, and his as well, and I was watching them making out in front of my eyes, I was wishing to be dead than before seeing all this. My heart broke into pieces, knowing the one I am going to marry does not care about me. I wanted to confront him, but I hear something they were discussing,

The lady asked Arjun-" when are you going to marry me, my king?

Arjun replied smiling-" Very soon, my dear, Once I become the king, I will marry that silly girl, and once I can have her for one night, all the powers, all the kingdom will be ours, then you shall be my queen.

The lady replied-" Is it really true? she has magical powers that she isn't aware of yet?

Arjun said-" Well it's a secret of the kingdom, we only have to find out, And Natasha, do not worry, Only you shall be my queen, Moreover, the way she insulted the future king, she shall be punished, I have planned everything.

I started wearing out of fear and disgust. the one I have always dreamt of being my man was a liar. he never loved me, It was all because of the throne. But what was the power he was talking about? I have to find out. I swept off my tears, I cannot be a weak person, I am the princes, the legal heir to the throne, I shall rise to be stronger. Enough of listening to others, Obeying without a question, NOw shall the time to wake up and know the truth.

Without wasting any time. I rode back to the castle,

Shaanti noticed something is wrong with me, She hurriedly came to me and asked. -" princess, I was worried about you. Is everything all right?

I replied coldly-" arrange a meeting in the king's court tomorrow morning.

She never heard me speaking so coldly, she left without a word, And I wanted for tomorrow's sunrise eagerly.

Blossoming in the meadows

Years passed by, the autumns leaves came and shredded its beautiful leaves, making the princess, more beautiful and rare, the winters were solace, to make her skin more pure than white, and the summer gave her the pleasant warmth of the summer heat, which makes her strong and radiant, and the energetic vernal equinox makes her joyful soul. Like this sixteen years passed by, the king and queen had protected their little daughter from the outside world. They didn't, let Megha, drop tears, they had made all her wishes fulfill to make her happy. Also, she was engaged to the son of the kingdom's official advisor's son, Knight, Arjun,

Princess Megha was admiring the meadows from her balcony while her best maid cum friend was doing her hair. Shaanti asked the princess:-"princess is looking for the knight? well, he went to nearby people, will take some time to come back.

I smiled and look back-" how do u know that shaanti?

Shaanti replied in a very prominent expression-" princess, I happened to be the head of the maids, nothing stays hidden from my ears!

I replied in a very joyful manner-" hmm.. this is why u are my favorite one. But when will he be back do you have any information?

Shaanti replied -" princess, as of I heard he will be back late. she looked a little worried. I quickly noticed and asked her back-"what happened? why do you seem that you want to tell me something and you cannot?

Shaanti looked down and replied-" please forgive me, princess, I don't want to make you worried, but I am not just only your maid, but your friend, I don't want you to see heartbroken!

"Heartbroken? tell me clearly shaanti !, you know I like straightforward answers and truth." I exclaimed.

Shaanti replied very calmly -" It's just that, Do you really love Arjun sir?

I looked to the windows and said-" Well do be honest I don't know what is love, Father and Mother had told me from childhood, he will be my husband one day, and mom told me he will always keep me safe and happy. Seeing my parents smile makes me really happy shaanti, I guess this is what called love. And as per Arjun, He always makes sure I stay happy, And I think Love takes slow and steady to be, hence, we have our whole life to love each other. But no one ever asked me what i really want ever. Well, let it go. But why do u ask this suddenly shaanti? Tell me what's going on.

Shaanti came front and hold princess's hand:- Princess, I really hope You find your love one days, and as per your parents, they love you unconditionally, and as Arjun sir, I don't want you to worried, But I got to hear, that in the northern part of the kingdom, the Hailo village, there is a girl who is...

Before she could finish her sentence, the queen came in.

Queen:-" My dear daughter, why aren't you ready yet? Arjun will be here by evening I heard of you better be ready by then. My daughter listens to me, men do not like to wait okay? It's we, who need to adjust to their time,

I simply acknowledged my mother and she exited. Shaanti left too, I was standing on my Window, and on my thoughts,

Since childhood, I have been taught to stand straight, talk politely, dressing etiquette like a royal family, How to become a future Queen, a better wife, a demure, and a fragile woman. I was taught to adjust, never to be spoken, a good lady doesn't do that. I never got love from a father, instead, I was taught by a king. Mother says I am a mature lady, with lots of responsibilities to serve the future. But somewhere inside me, there is still that little girl, wondering how does it feel to fly, how does the world look outside this castle, This kingdom, she wants to explore, to lead, to fall in love. But she wasn't allowed to. Well to this boundary, they cannot hold one thing, i actually secretly use to go outside this castle sometimes. Just around the southern border of our kingdom, besides the valley, there is a small abandoned temple of Lord Shiva, beside the huge tree. I come here sometimes when I feel sad or torment by being in that big castle listening always what to do, how to do. and where to do. Shaanti and Arjun only know that I come and visit here.

Besides shaanti, Arjun is my childhood friend. he saved me many times from my father earlier. But what he thinks of me, is I am his little queen, weak and sometimes need to pamper that's all. But yes we had a bond.

Here, in the temple, I forget all my responsibilities, all my sorrow, and can be myself. I worship Lord Shiva so that someday he might listen to me, and help me to get from my sorrow. I just sit around the tree and admired the beauty of nature.

Today, I escaped again to the temple, and while returning, it was almost evening and I saw from the far it was Arjun. About Arjun, He was a wise man. The knight and the leader of the soldier of Rajnagri. My father's favorite like son, Successor to the throne as a King, and my would-be husband.

Arjun approached me and said-" Greetings princess, now where are you coming from?

I smiled and greets him-" Good evening Arjun, I was returning to the castle from the temple.

Arjun Take my hand and took me on the horse while riding he asked again in a sarcastic tone-" Now what made you escape the castle again princess? Don't you know it's not safe to be here, and especially for being my Queen, it won't suit you now?

I looked at him in a bit confused and asked-" But you never stopped me before coming here. You know this is a place I feel little myself from the closed doors of the castle.

he did not give any expression and replied -" It was before when I was crowned as the future King and You being announced as my future wife. Grow up, Princess. You will have responsibilities to carry on as my wife. And If you want to come here, I will make arrangements from now, You will be accompanied by the soldiers and maids.

I did not answer anything and stayed mum. He Looked and noticed me being a little grumpy. So he asked one again in his usual cold voice-" Now is that the angry face I see of my future queen? What happened?

I think twice, before speaking out,-" We are friends before being husband and wife right?

He replied in a puzzled tone-" Of course

I looked away and asked him-" is that mean I can ask you a question and you would reply to me honestly?

he wore a proud smile and replied-" Do u doubt princess?

I said-" No it's just that, I have been hearing few rumors' about you, that worried me a little bit, that there may be some other girl at the Hailo village, in the northern part of the kingdom, where you visit often.

Arjun stopped the horse, and looked at me in a bit harsh way-" Are you doubting me? Do You dare doubt your future king?

I replied softly-" No, I don't want to, but there was rumor's all around

He harshly replied to me-" And that is a rumor princess, do not be fooled by it. You are the future queen of this kingdom, and soon to be my wife. rather than listening to these stupid rumors, your part of the job is to maintain the Harem and take care of me and think about our future generation. Your father wouldn't be much happy to know that his daughter is escaping the castle, bothered about the mere rumors, and questioning the future King.

I understood, I was stopped again being speaking of my mind. Tears rolled in the corner of my eyes and I tried holding it off so Arjun couldn't see that. I was not sad that he talked harshly, I was actually sad that my childhood friend has somewhere disappeared into the future king. And I acknowledged him-" I Understood, and I will follow it further.

He rode the horse without saying a word. And we stopped near the palace.

Into the woods

Everything has changed, I have never imagined my life would turn into something like this, Though I was fond of adventure since my childhood, now, I am scared, Scared to explore, or scared to face my destiny, that's hard to explain. I have grown in the royal family, where I have always been taught, the princess shall be in grace to become a queen, Gentle and kind to people and mankind, and shall always have the potentiality to settle her own family. Princesses do not go out and fight, Princesses shall not go out alone, And their King is the only one man in her life. I was engaged at a very young age, though I had never understood the meaning of love with Arjun, I accepted the fact that he shall be the one I would spend my rest of the life. Usually on my birthday, every year my parents celebrate it very huge, It is the day when I was officially allowed to go out of the palace with my parents and Arjun been there with me to see and meet the people of my kingdom, they use to give me lots of presents as much as they can give. It used to be a happy time. But this birthday has changed everything in my life. The person I use to think to spend my life with has turned to be someone who broke my heart. I fled from my own kingdom to seek the truth and lost somewhere I am not aware of, My kingdom got attacked and I was not sure if I could meet my mother, father, or Shaanti or anyone ever again. And today I had no idea what happened, How did all that happen, and what was actually that about, Is Arjun really speaking the truth? Do I have any special powers I was not aware of? Is it why my parents never wanted me to go out much? But why? And how do I have these powers? how do I control them? And then suddenly I can see the man I saw yesterday, in his bright knight Armor, he walked towards me and stopped, he smiled and offered his hands, he said-" Trust me, will you?"

and then I woke up, I realized I was dreaming, all this was in my head, I looked around and I realized I was on the horse, I looked beside, I found him, With his dignity, he is carrying me off, For a minute, everything stopped around me, I remember what I saw in my dream he asked-" Trust me, will you?" Will I? I don't know? I don't even know him? Should I? But why does it feel so safe around him? Wait I remember I saw before I blacked out, He also has some magical powers he protected himself from my powers. Will he help me? Then it hit me, Where does he taking me to? I got all my nerves back and asked him to stop.

I said-" STOP!!!! where are you taking me?

He glared at me and didn't bother and continued to go further.

I said-" Wait, Where are you taking me? Tell me, Take me back to my kingdom now. Or else you saw I have powers I will use on you too.

He did not bother again to my words and kept moving, it was pissing me off, I Slide down from the horse, And took the sword which was kept on the left side of the horse, and hold onto him firmly. He smiled and finally, I got his attention. He smiled at me and said-" princess! No need for that, Keep it down, We don't want you to have any trouble"

I looked at him with a confused face I said-" What do you mean by I will be in trouble? Mr. You are not taking me seriously I see.

He kept walking with the horse towards the forest. This makes me so angry and anxious that why isn't he afraid of me? Is he taking me for granted? Do-Do I look weak? I need to look strong before him, to make sure, he is scared of me. I pulled up the sword again and with a confident face and hold it in front of him. He put down my sword and looked at me and said-" Princess If I had to kill you I would have done long back. Instead, you are here alive, Thanks to me.

I looked at him in utter shock and said-" Thanks to you? I don't even know you. I ran away from my kingdom in search of the truth and got trapped here!!! My fiancé turned to my enemy overnight!! I am lost in this dark forest, I don't know how I killed those people there!! You are kidnapping me and I should thank you? really? Tell me where are you taking me to? How are you? I demand the truth now!!!"

He stopped at once and looked at me with his cold face and said-" ran away? So you are the princess my mother is looking for?"

I replied in a confused face-" Your mother is looking for me? why?"

With his expressionless face, he said-" That I have to find out yet. Till then you are safe with me."

I don't know why I want to believe him, I fell for his every word, For some reason, He does not seem to be an unknown person, so without any further words I followed him, within some time, we reached the darkest part of the forest, there was the castle, Looks like his home, He took the other way in and we reached to a basement. He turned towards me-" This is where you will stay, help yourself. If you need anything... Don't bother me."

Well, that was rude of him, But he did help me But why? Well without thinking much, I told him-" Why are you helping me?"

He turned back and looked at my eyes he said in a hushed voice-" That is yet to find out princess, But until I get to know why my mother wants you, You stay here, I hope you will get everything here. And one more thing, do not leave this room at any cause, and for your safety, do not tell where you are from okay?

I said-" Okay but what if they ask me about where I am from?"

He turned around and said-" tell them you are prince Sanjay's guest, They will not bother you anymore."

I said-" Thank you for saving me,"

He said while he was leaving-" We will see about that.

After he left, Two maids came over and helped me change. Then I realized I hot few hurts from the fight we had. Also, I feel very weak. So after I changed up, I fell asleep. I woke up the next day in the morning and saw a princess in my room, looking around. I excused myself and come towards her, in fear who is she and why is she here? Prince said I must not reveal my true identity, I was thinking what to say, In that time, she came towards me with a proud smile and told me-" You must be the new toy of his highness, And you are wondering who am I? well my dear I am prince Sanjay's fiancé Princess Sayantika. Do not feel that you are in this palace that means he is thinking of any future with you. It's just for few days. So I am here to tell you, you must know your place and try not to think and hurt yourself. U must know he does not belong any heart"

I was listening to her in complete silence all this time and couldn't understand much, other than she was his fiancé, and he had many affairs and she was thinking I am another one of his conquests. I wanted to tell her this is all a lie, I do not want to involve even with someone like this, But I thought to keep silent, It is for the best, I just nodded my head in her reply.

She left telling me-" Enjoy your few days here"

After she left, I took a deep breath and looked from the window, It is nothing like Rajnagri. The sun does not fall on the ground much, it is weirdly cold around here and cloudy. It is dark and shady and scary. I wonder what kind of people live here in this dark forest. But it came to my mind, I must not think that much, rather I should see how I can escape from here. I know he told me he will get me back but I cannot utterly rely on some stranger. So I decided I would search my own ways. It was the time of the afternoon, mostly every maid outside my room are somewhere else, it looks like a good time to see around if I can escape. I took one of the maids' dress and cover my face with the cloth and took the west side, and start walking towards, and soon after some time I stopped hearing a voice, it seems a known voice. It looks like the Queen's chamber, It was big and with many guards and her voice, Sayantika's. they were talking about Rajnagri!!! I wonder why they are talking about my kingdom, Well Sanjay did tell me his mother wants me, but I didn't know why. So I decided to hear the conversation. I hide behind the big door, without being noticed by the guards and started listening.

The first voice said-" What have you bring news for me today my dear?

Sayantika said-" Her majesty, Prince bought a new girl today, I was coming from there.

The voice told her-" My dear, you are the future queen of this kingdom you must not get affected with these little things, tell me the news I wanted to hear.

sayantika replied-" Forgive me her majesty, I was a little selfish, Yes I managed to get information about the princess, After our soldiers attacked the kingdom, she fled to the same old man we were looking for, but before she reached him, she disappeared from there. But I reached to the old man on time and got his words, She is born on the 9th celestial birth realm. So she possesses powerful magical powers that she is not aware of, she possesses the power of life, water. One of the ancient blessings from the god's power. She was blessed and very powerful. But she does not know about her powers yet. But since it is her 17th birthday, she already had unlocked her destiny.

The voice turned into deep-" She must be powerful, but she is naive, and with such powers, I can become the most powerful devil on earth."

Sayantika replied-" Her majesty I do not understand."

The voice said-" you don't have to, Tell Daniel to Kill every one of Rajnagri and bring me that girl as soon as possible."

I was shocked that I was trapped in the palace that attacked my kingdom, and wants to get my powers, They want to kill my people and me. How can I save them, I have magical powers but I don't know how to use them. No, I cannot just wait here. He fooled me, He knew from the start. He lied. I must return to save my people.

So without wasting much time, I came back to my room, and I was so scared and anxious I started panicking, What should I do? Just then Sanjay entered my room and in panic, I hold the sword to him-" Why did you bring me here? why do you want to attack my kingdom? What have they done to you? I beg you please let me go.

He in his confused state said-" what are you talking about?

He came towards me. I hold the sword firm and said-" Do not dare to lie. You have a fiancé, and I heard someone talking here today with your fiancé, you want my powers. But trust me, I don't know anything about my powers. I...

He looked at me firmly and come forth, the sword started hurting his chest and started bleeding but he kept his eyes on me, he said-" Is it bothering you, my fiancé?

I said-' What? No!!! Just let me go...

He said looking at my eyes-" princess, I do not want to harm you, And I did not know about your kingdom. Mother told me about this today, and trust me, I don't know maybe you don't know about me yet, But I do not want you to get harmed. I promise. U can trust me.

I said-" Trust you? Your fiancé said you don't have a heart, and mistook me as one of your mistresses. I...

He came towards me and said-" Princess, This is even the first time for me, but I promise you no one can hurt you. You are safe here. Tomorrow there is a party, so a good time for us to leave. stay ready. He left without any further word. And I trusted him once again and waited for tomorrow.

Identity

The very next morning, I woke up and was waiting in my room, when two maids came inside and handed me over a beautiful red gown, I asked them in a confusion-" what is this all for?"

Just then, a young man came inside and smiled at me he said-" Well, everybody was telling the truth, I see."

I said-" I beg your pardon, I do not understand, And if I may ask who are you?"

He replied with a smile-" So my brothers' new mistress is not only beautiful but also dare to speak inside the castle. Tell me one thing miss, are you not afraid to be here?

I understood he is Sanjay's brother. I said-" I am sorry I am new here, so I do not know people from here Prince,"

He said-" you may call me Tarun."

I smiled and accepted his term. I said-" Well Tarun, it was nice to talk with you. But I don't understand why is this gown for?"

Tarun replied to me-" Being my brother's mistress, you don't know that today is his birthday? That's new."

I said-" Oh yes, I have heard about today's party but I didn't know about the occasion."

He frowned and glared at me for few seconds then he asked me-" Which part of the kingdom are you from?"

I started stammering-" I... I..."

In the meantime, Sanjay came there he replied-'"She is from the southern part. But why my brother is suddenly concerned about that today?

Tarun looked at Sanjay and smiled at him, he said-" Good morning brother, I didn't mean to interrupt, It just comes to my mind, She does not seem familiar with this kingdom, Hence I intend to ask her ."

Sanjay replied with a keen look on him-" Yes she is not familiar because She grew up outside this kingdom, and yet to learn a lot, But I don't think my brother needs to know further than this, She will greet the queen accordingly Since I am here She is my responsibility."

Tarun turned stoned and replied-" Sure brother."

He left with a glance at me, At least Sanjay saved me this time. I saw he was leaving I stopped him and said-"Thank you for saving me once again"

He said-" Mention not princess"

I replied again-" Happy birthday Sanjay, I didn't know."

He looked at me and replied-" you can make it up by your presence at the party tonight."

I said in a worried tone-" But lots of people going to be there... and"

He looked with a keen eye-" And?"

I said-" People are already thinking of me as your mistress, I don't want to offend your fiance anymore."

He comes closer to me and said in a hushed tone-" What are you bothered of? being my mistress or with my fiance?

I got nervous by his closeness, I said-" I am not bothered at all!!!"

He smiled and said-" Then see you at the party tonight don't worry it is a mask party, and yes, Don't get bothered by people, they are jealous because you are beautiful."

I don't know why, he makes me blush. He left from there, and I thought to be there for him, because at least that I can do as a gratitude to him for saving me.

In the evening, I got ready in the red gown, made my hair, and wear a mask. I was a little nervous because I almost got a close encounter with Tarun in the morning, also Sayantika did not like me very much either, but still, I took a deep breath and walked down the stairs. All eyes were on me, probably wondering who am I or as they were thanking me as the prince's mistress. But yet I dare to walk down, I noticed Tarun looking at me, he came forth to welcome me, and in the meantime, Sanjay came and hold my hand. He took me to the dance floor. While we were dancing, all eyes were on us, He holds my hands, Pulled me closer, his left hands on my waist and he was closer than he should be. My heart started racing so fast, I blushed. I noticed that and smiled at me, He said-" Glad I could make you blush"

I came to my senses and replied-" flirting? You know that I am your enemy right?"

He smiled and whispered in my ears-" Not mine princess, Of my kingdom's"

I frowned and replied-' And how does both make a difference?"

He smiled and replied to me-" I don't like queen's work, I don't interfere on her kingdom, I am just me,"King of kings", Sanjay"

I said-" you are crazy"

He said-" I kind of like it"

I smiled and replied-" So it's true of what I am hearing, The crown prince is good with girls?"

He managed a glance around the hall and replied-" So they dare to talk about my reputation here huh?"

I said-" truth always comes around"

He seemed to ignore that topic and looked at me in confidence and said-"So let's be friends?

I thought about it sometime and replied-"Friends", I paused for sometimes and asked him again-" So, what I heard is true?"

He replied with a serious look-" What did you hear?"

I said-" You play with women's heart?" He did not reply anything, I asked him again-" What if someone really falls for you?

He replied with a stoned face-" I don't know, I am just finding..."

I replied-" Finding what?"

He said-" someone whom I can love maybe, someone who can give me a heart."

I can feel he is hiding something from me, I asked him-" What are you hiding from me? what secret do you hold?"

He replied in a serious face-" Nothing, why do you think that?"

I said-" Sanjay I am here for five days, I have been listening to few things about this kingdom, Like this kingdom never been on any affairs outside this kingdom, always hiding something, No one has ever seen the queen, and I kept feeling something is a mystery in this kingdom."

While we were talking about all this just then the Queen arrives, Everyone bows down against her. She was tall, pale white, in a dark black gown, Looks absolutely evil. Sayantika comes forth and greets her. Queen Diana looked around and spotted Sanjay with me. She looked back at Syantika and whispered her something. She stands upstairs in the gallery and Announced-"Greetings to my people, today I am very happy that you all are present on my son's birthday. But today I have a very special announcement, as you know, Sanjay is the crown prince of Devgarh, Today I announce my Son, Sanjay's and Sayantika's marriage. By the very next month, shall be the marriage. I hope you all will wish them a good future."

Everyone Clap on the announcement. Sayantika and Queen Diana seemed happy, but Sanjay looked a little bit awkward. He left from there without saying anything. Honestly, I wasn't happy either with the news. I don't know why I felt to go with him, Ask him why isn't he happy? I was about to leave when Tarun came there.

He smiled and asked my hand-" May I have one dance?

Out of courtesy, I said-" Sure"

While we start dancing, he asked me-" well, In the kingdom of the dead, a girl so lively like you is a mystery, but where are you from you said?"

I stammered-" I...I... uh..."

he said-" We will let it go, Tell me when did you come to this palace?"

I replied-" Five days ago"

He looked at me with keen eyes he said-" Hmm... You know how this is so relatable, we found a few of our soldiers killed in the woods on the same day. And there was this princess, from Rajnagri who was missing from that exact day... do you think it is relatable somehow?

I got a little bit scared I don't know what to answer him, and just then Sanjay hoped in there. he said looking at Tarun with a glare-" I would like to have her back, she is mine"

Tarun smiled and said-" Yes brother, I know she is yours, because whatever in this kingdom is, yours."

Tarun left from there, And Sanjay took me to my room. He said we need to leave as soon as possible. He said-" Princess, we have thirty minutes, we leave"

I said in a panic-" I think Tarun is guessing my identity."

Sanjay said-" I know, Don't worry, I will keep you safe. Do you trust me?

I said looking at his eyes-" Yes I do"

As per our conversation, We meet outside the castle,

He said-" You ready?

I replied-" Yes"

Just then Tarun reached there with few guards, He smiled at me and said-" Hello Megha!!! Princess of Rajnagri."

Sanjay said-" Tarun, Leave from here, she is my guest"

Tarun smiled at his words and replied-" Dear brother, She is our enemy, Mother demands to see her, So I am here, to take her."

Sanjay replied-' She is not going anywhere"

Tarun said-" Brother, You know, you are favorite of the mother, But I have always had to fight for my rights and love from her, So today I shall take her. It's the queen's order. And you dare not ignore that.

Sanjay looked at me, He said-" Megha, RUN!!!"

I started running towards the forest, While Sankjay was fighting against Tarun and the soldiers. He used his powers against them. While for a few minutes the soldiers were falling weak against him, he ran towards me, Just then Tarun came from behind me and attacked me, Sanjay threw his sword towards me, and I started fighting, I was getting on Tarun's nerve. Just then Few more soldiers came there. Sanjay came beside me, He holds my hand, and just then, our magic worked. It creates a guard against us, and everyone falls hard on the ground. Seeing the opportunity, we ran towards the woods.

The Chase

The door opened and the rays of the lights fall on the ground, my eyes were seeking the person I wanted to see, But I knew it would be impossible, how can he come here? So will I die here? Will, I never can express my love? will I never see him again? and then, I saw a manly figure comes inside, and as the light, lights up there It was Sanjay.

I screamed in joy-" Sanjay, Is that really you? Am I dreaming?

He comes to me in a hurry he said-"No, you are not, and yes Megha, how can I not?"

He began to untie my hands, while I asked-" How did you found me? How did you know I am here?'

He said-" Don't worry about that, as of now, we need to leave"

I said-" wait, your mother...'

He said-" I know"

He released me, and we ran towards the door, and what I saw next, shocked me. We were in a cave, which was under the deep sea, It was protected by a black magic spell, hidden from the outside world, This is where she hides her all truth. Sanjay looked at me and asked-" Do you trust me?"

I said-" Yes"

he grabbed my waist and with his magical powers, he pulled us out from there and we reached above a cliff. He said-" now let's go...

I said-" wait, you lied to me, you are not..."

He looked deep into my eyes and said-" not a human? yes, I am not a human? I don't have a soul, and I don't have a heart but..." He comes closer to me and took my hand and kept in my chest, he said-" Did you feel that? My heart beats in your heart. you are the living being in my life Megha!!! and I live within you. The day we first met, when you activated your magical powers and it touched mine, I felt the presence of my heartbeat within you."

Tears come in my eyes and I knew he is the one, my heart belongs to. I said-" Sanjay, I..."

Before I could finish, Tarun appeared with his soldiers. Sanjay took my hand and we started running to the north, We almost reached the border of Devgarh, and in the meantime, Queen Diana and Sayantika appeared there and we were surrounded by the guards.

The queen looked with an angry face towards Sanjay-" Sanjay, you have disappointed me, I did not expect that my own son will lie to me for this silly girl"

Sanjay plead before the queen, Diana-" Mother please, Let her go"

The queen replied-" My dear son, I loved you, I have given you everything you have ever wanted, and probably every other person wished for. I gave you powers, rank, throne, Excepted all your silly wishes. Still, you intend to choose this silly girl over your mother? I am very disappointed."

Sanjay said-" Mother please, My heart belongs to her"

The Queen roared in anger-" You don't have a heart Sanjay."

Sayantika went closer to Sanjay, she said-" My prince, this girl made chaos to Devgarh, Let's not argue further, let us go home" Sanjay pulled out his hands from her. He looked to Queen in pleading eyes.

Queen ignored him and looked at me, she said-"This girl needs to die, I need her power to become the ultimatum, and then there will be no one to stand before me."

I looked at Sanjay, he was caught in the spell not able to move, Trying hard to get out from there. Tarun with his soldiers was ready to fight with me, Sayantika had a confident face, thinking, Sanjay would return to him. And Queen Diana was just standing there looking at his son, in pain. She lost her humanity, for magical powers. And Sanjay was getting weak for her. I had to do something, But I knew I couldn't win them alone. I looked at Sanjay, with tears in my eyes, I said-" Listen to me Sanjay, I came back for you, to tell you that I love you, my heart belongs to you. And at least I am happy that I could see you before I die."

Sanjay replied in a blank face-" you are not going to die. Use your powers, Save yourself"

I replied smiling-" How can I leave you? I love you, I take the responsibility, Till the last breath could make us separate."

I created A magical force within me, and I took out Sanjay's beating heart, Which I stole from the queen's den, I knew, it still has humanity left within, but has lots of dark spells around, Without thinking much, I started giving out my magical power of life to his heart, It was almost done while Soldiers were attacking me from the outside of the force, The queen roared-" NO!!!". She used her black magical spell on me, and the forced break, The spell starts choking me, But somehow, I managed to restore the heart into him. He was no longer controlled by the queen, he is no longer weak, He broke the queen's spell, and came out, he starts fighting against the soldiers, With no bound of his powers, he became stronger. Sayantika tried to stop him, and he slashed her to the ground, Tarun came back from her, and his swords pinned him to the tree, his hands got hurt, but he managed to escape, in the rage of his anger he created the sixth form of fire that can perish one's soul. and within no time, he killed Tarun, the soldiers got sacred and slide away from him. the queen saw all the action and got furious. She holds the powers on me, to choke enough for me to die. Sanjay took his sword to fight with the queen, She easily got Sanjay and brought him down with another hand.

She smiled and said-" What makes you think you are stronger than me? You silly boy, You got your humanity back, that means, you became weak, I am the devil herself, you dare to put your sword against me?"

She took his sword and put it in his heart, he started screaming in pain I looked at the queen and begged her-"No please, He is your son"

She looked at me in her red eyes-" No one is mine, other than the powers" she said.

I said-" Please, Please kill me, kill me, let him go please, I beg you"

She ignored me and tighten the grip on both hands, one to choke me and another to kill Sanjay, She said-' You both must die now"

she kept hurting Sanjay with her powers, Which made me inflamed, and without my knowledge, I engaged my inner soul to connect with the energy and forms the weapon, I put my soul as the part of the weapon and attacked Queen Diana. My powers were pure and powerful than her. I attacked her soul and hit on the point. Her body was a form of burned ashes like dark, and I was the form of life, The purity of my power turned her into a stone. And finally, she died. After a fight of eternity, We finally got rid of the darkness, But then I looked at Sanjay, he was badly hurt, I had to save him. But I had already used half of my soul to kill queen Diana, I was too weak to save him, But I could not let him die, So I connect my soul with his, and gave my powers to save him. I fell to the ground with tears in my eyes, looking at Sanjay,

Sanjay was saved but was badly hurt to move around, He cried out loud-" NO MEGHA NO!!!!"

He fell to the ground and blacked out. And I moved my hands towards him, Hoping to touch him Before I die. My whole life turned upside down, I lost my friend, my fiancé turned into my enemy, lost my parents, my kingdom, I couldn't lose my love, So to prove my love for him, I gave up my other soul to him. And the sunsets there.